ROBOT POWER!

by Celeste Sisler

illustrated by Dave Aikins

based on the teleplay "Robot Power!"
by Morgan von Ancken & Halcyon Person

Random House 🏠 New York

Buzz. Clink. Tap.
Blaze and AJ hear
noises coming from
Axle City Garage.

Gabby is making a robot!

Blaze throws a ball.
Gabby codes
the robot
to chase it!
Beep! Boop! Bop!

Pickle and Crusher
see the little robot
zip by.

Crusher feels left out.
He wants to make
some robots!

Crusher builds
a chomping robot,
a throwing robot,
and a big blasting robot!

Oh, no!
Crusher's robots
smash through
a wall.

The robots
run wild in Axle City!
Blaze has
to stop them.

14

AJ and Gabby
design, build,
and code.
Blaze becomes
Robot Blaze!

The chomping robot
is hungry.
Blaze throws him
a metal bar.
Chomp! Chomp!

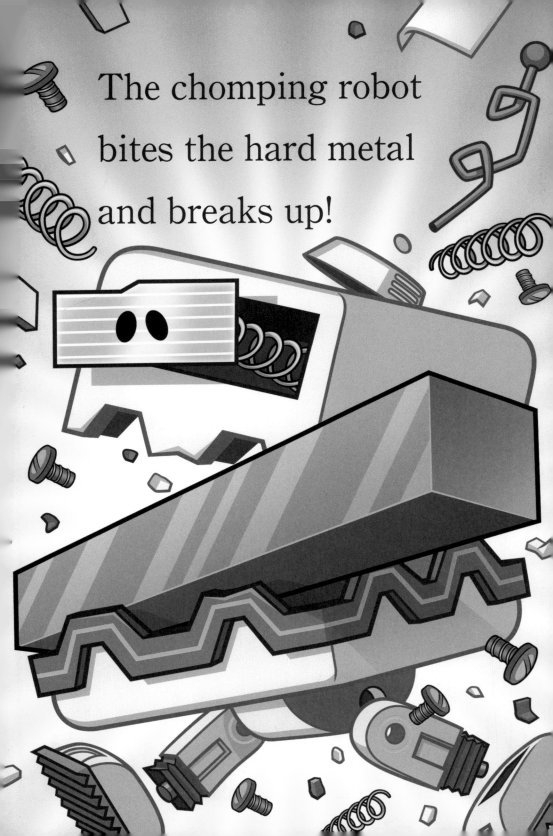

The chomping robot bites the hard metal and breaks up!

The throwing robot
is making a mess.
Robot Blaze
to the rescue!

Blaze tosses a log.
The throwing robot
trips over it—
and falls apart!

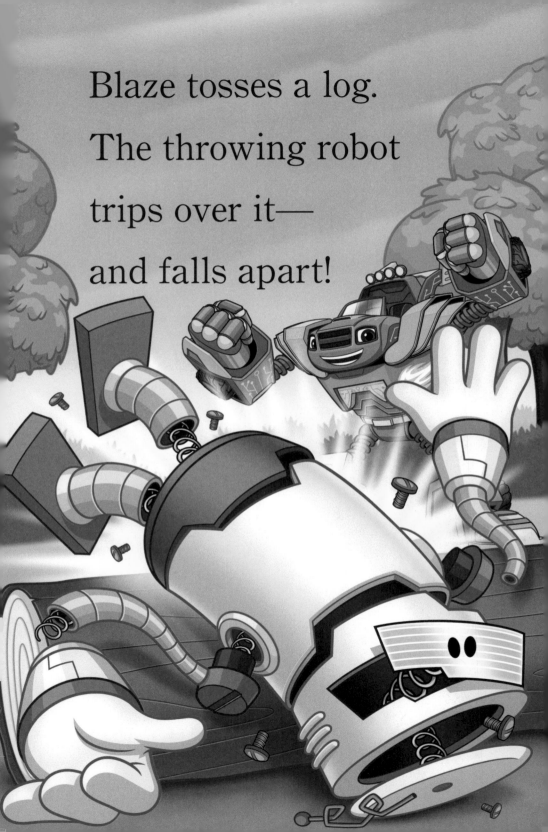

The blasting robot
is also making a mess.
Who will stop him?

Gabby and AJ have a plan.
They tell Robot Blaze
to use Blazing Speed!

Robot Blaze uses
Blazing Speed
to block the blaster!

Smash!

The blasting robot

falls apart.

Robot Blaze saves the day!
His friends
cheer for him.
Hooray!